The Adventures of Max and Pinky

BEST BUDS

by

Maxwell Eaton III

Alfred A. Knopf New York

To the 'Rents!

THIS IS A BORZOI BOOK PUBLISHED BY ALFRED A. KNOPF

Published in the United States by Alfred A. Knopf, an imprint of Random House Children's Books,
a division of Random House, Inc., New York.

KNOPF, BORZOI BOOKS, and the colophon are registered trademarks of Random House, Inc.

www.randomhouse.com/kids

Educators and librarians, for a variety of teaching tools, visit us at
www.randomhouse.com/teachers

Library of Congress Cataloging-in-Publication Data
Eaton, Maxwell.
Best buds / Maxwell Eaton III. — 1st ed.
p. cm. — (The adventures of Max and Pinky)
SUMMARY: Best friends Max and Pinky have an adventure together every Saturday, but one week Max looks
everywhere and cannot find Pinky.
ISBN 978-0-375-83803-3 (trade) — ISBN 978-0-375-93803-0 (lib. bdg.)
[1. Best friends—Fiction. 2. Friendship—Fiction. 3. Hide-and-seek—Fiction.]
I. Title. II. Series: Eaton, Maxwell. Adventures of Max and Pinky.
PZ7.E3892Bes 2007
[E]—dc22
2006002037

The illustrations in this book were created using black pen-and-ink with digital coloring.

MANUFACTURED IN CHINA
10 9 8 7 6 5 4 3 2 1
First Edition

Max and Pinky are best buds.

Max and Pinky love adventure.

Hey, where did the marshmallows go?

They go here.

They go up.

Sometimes Max does one thing...

while Pinky does another.

Today is Saturday.
But where is Pinky?

Max decides to search
Pinky's favorite places.

He looks in the gooey
brown mud puddle.

He asks around the big red barn.

Max is so worried. Where can Pinky be?
Oh no! What if he's . . . .

Lost in the woods?

Or carried away by bunnies!

Where can he be? Think, Max!

Aha!

BUSTED!

Max and Pinky are best buds.

Always have been.

Always will be.